DATE DUE

A Treeful of Pigs

ARNOLD LOBEL

A Treeful of Pigs

PICTURES BY ANITA LOBEL

GREENWILLOW BOOKS
A DIVISION OF WILLIAM MORROW & COMPANY, INC., NEW YORK

LIBRARY OF CONGRESS CATALOGING IN PUBLICATION DATA
'LOBEL, ARNOLD.   A TREEFUL OF PIGS.
SUMMARY: A FARMER'S WIFE USES DRASTIC MEASURES
TO GET HER HUSBAND TO ABANDON HIS LAZY WAYS.
[1. LAZINESS—FICTION] I. LOBEL, ANITA. II. TITLE PZ7.L7795TR
[E]   78-1810   ISBN 0-688-80177-3   ISBN 0-688-84177-5 LIB. BDG.

For Emily, Stephen,
and Adam Raphael,
with love

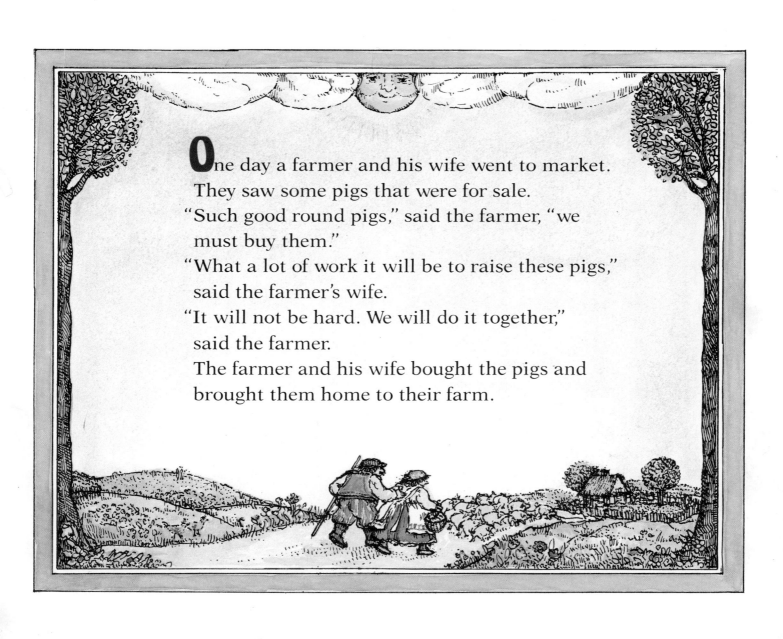

One day a farmer and his wife went to market.
They saw some pigs that were for sale.
"Such good round pigs," said the farmer, "we
must buy them."
"What a lot of work it will be to raise these pigs,"
said the farmer's wife.
"It will not be hard. We will do it together,"
said the farmer.
The farmer and his wife bought the pigs and
brought them home to their farm.

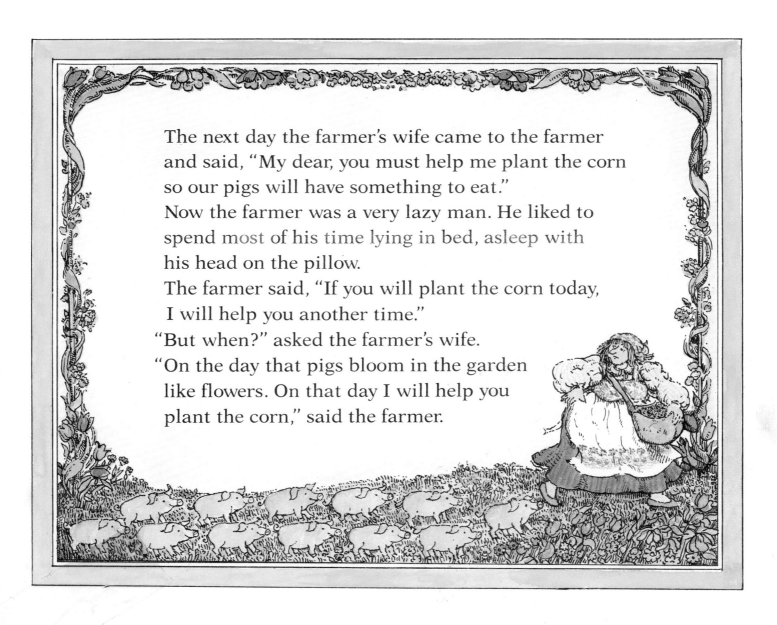

The next day the farmer's wife came to the farmer and said, "My dear, you must help me plant the corn so our pigs will have something to eat."

Now the farmer was a very lazy man. He liked to spend most of his time lying in bed, asleep with his head on the pillow.

The farmer said, "If you will plant the corn today, I will help you another time."

"But when?" asked the farmer's wife.

"On the day that pigs bloom in the garden like flowers. On that day I will help you plant the corn," said the farmer.

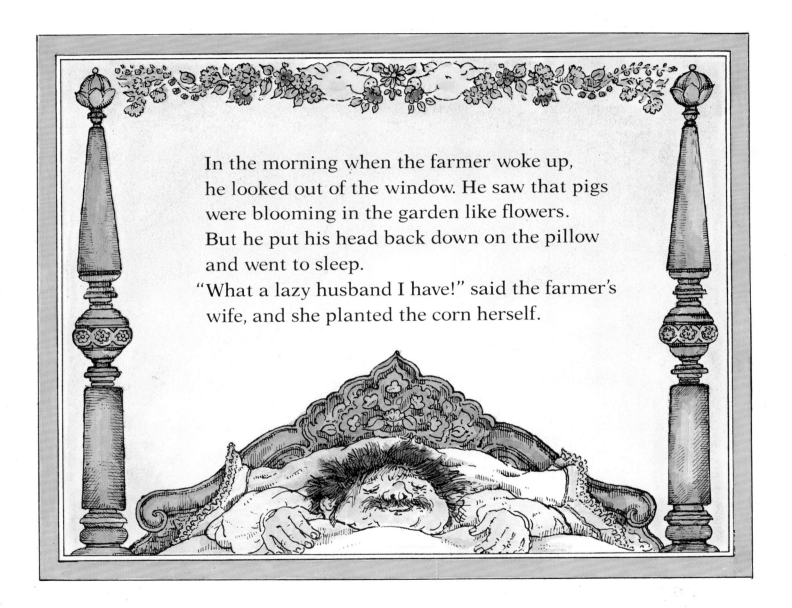

In the morning when the farmer woke up,
he looked out of the window. He saw that pigs
were blooming in the garden like flowers.
But he put his head back down on the pillow
and went to sleep.
"What a lazy husband I have!" said the farmer's
wife, and she planted the corn herself.

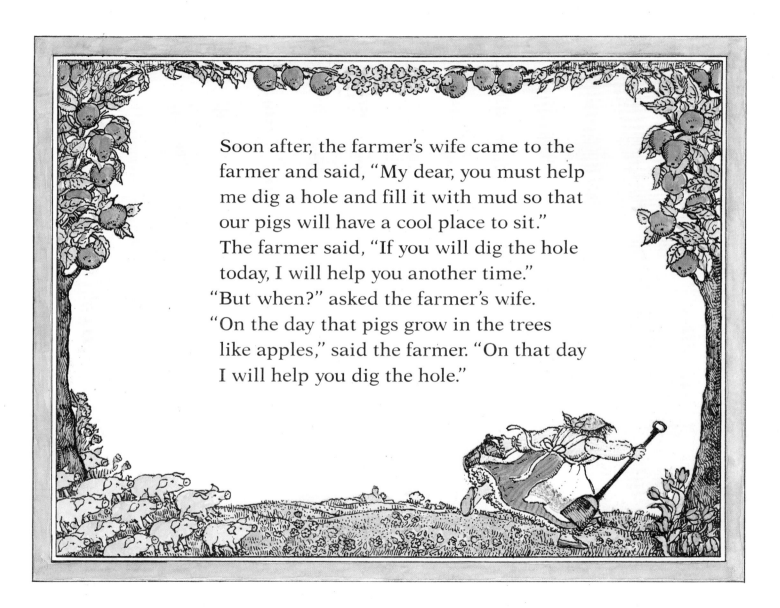

Soon after, the farmer's wife came to the
farmer and said, "My dear, you must help
me dig a hole and fill it with mud so that
our pigs will have a cool place to sit."
The farmer said, "If you will dig the hole
today, I will help you another time."
"But when?" asked the farmer's wife.
"On the day that pigs grow in the trees
like apples," said the farmer. "On that day
I will help you dig the hole."

In the morning when the farmer woke up, he looked out of the window. He saw that pigs were growing in the trees like apples. But he put his head back down on the pillow and went to sleep.

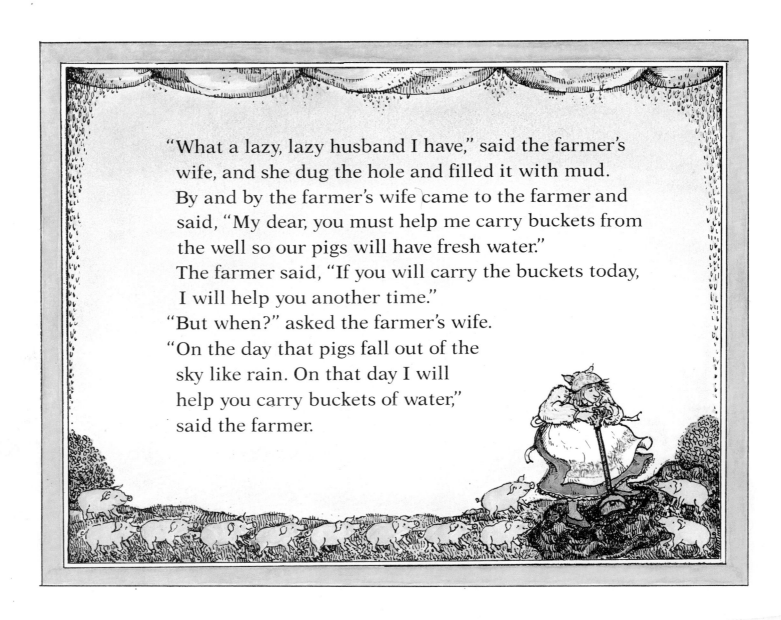

"What a lazy, lazy husband I have," said the farmer's
wife, and she dug the hole and filled it with mud.
By and by the farmer's wife came to the farmer and
said, "My dear, you must help me carry buckets from
the well so our pigs will have fresh water."
The farmer said, "If you will carry the buckets today,
I will help you another time."
"But when?" asked the farmer's wife.
"On the day that pigs fall out of the
sky like rain. On that day I will
help you carry buckets of water,"
said the farmer.

In the morning when the farmer woke up, he looked out of the window. He saw that pigs were falling out of the sky like rain. But he put his head back down on the pillow and went to sleep.

"What a lazy, lazy, lazy husband I have," said the farmer's wife, and she carried the buckets of water from the well herself.

When the corn was ripe, the farmer's wife came to the farmer and said, "My dear, you must help me harvest the corn so our pigs will have a fine dinner."

But the farmer yawned and said, "I wish the day would come when those pigs would disappear like the snow in the spring. On that day I will really rest well."

In the morning when the farmer woke up,
he looked out of the window. He did not see
the pigs anywhere. They were not blooming
in the garden like flowers. They were not
growing in the trees like apples. They were
not falling out of the sky like rain. They had
disappeared like the snow in the spring.
"What have I done?" cried the farmer.
"What has happened to our wonderful pigs?"

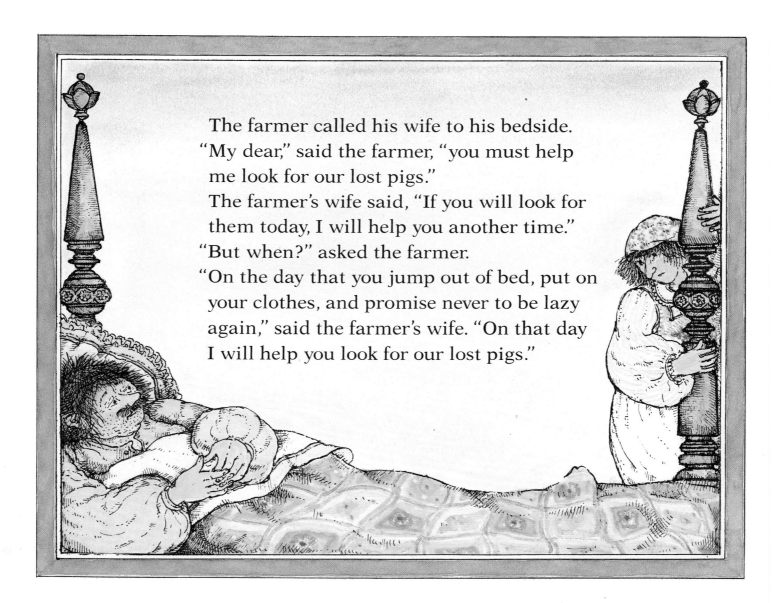

The farmer called his wife to his bedside.
"My dear," said the farmer, "you must help
me look for our lost pigs."
The farmer's wife said, "If you will look for
them today, I will help you another time."
"But when?" asked the farmer.
"On the day that you jump out of bed, put on
your clothes, and promise never to be lazy
again," said the farmer's wife. "On that day
I will help you look for our lost pigs."

The farmer quickly jumped out of bed.
He put on his shirt and his pants and
his boots. He fell on his knees and cried,
"I will never, never be lazy again!"
"Good enough," said the farmer's wife.

The farmer's wife ran outside
and opened the cellar door.
All of the pigs came bouncing
out into the sunshine.

The farmer helped his wife harvest
the corn. He helped her cook the meal.
Then the farmer, the farmer's wife and
the pigs sat down to a delicious dinner
of corn pudding and hot corn muffins.

On that day the farmer promised
always to keep his promise,
and from that day on he did.